The Lukewarm Church

Godwin E Morka

ISBN: 9798839723832

Cover design & Interior Layout: Oluwaseyi A. Alade

❧ DEDICATION ☙

Dedicated to those who have embraced the Grace of God and whose anointing is infectious to people around them.

"I know your works, that you are neither cold nor hot. I could wish you were cold or hot. So then, because you are lukewarm, and neither cold nor hot, I will vomit you out of my mouth"

Revelations Chapter 3:15-16

ஐ CONTENTS ଔ

ℬ ACKNOWLEDGMENTS ℛ

I would like to appreciate with gratitude the invaluable spiritual training I have received over the years from notable men of God, especially Pastor Olusegun Abiodun Longe, General Overseer Emeritus of Upper Room Baptist Church, Lagos, who instilled in me the discipline of Bible Study (2 Timothy Chapter 3, verse 16). The ministries of Brother Gbile Akanni, late Revered Moses Rahaman Popoola, Sunday Isehunwa and a host of others also have stoked in me the zeal to study the word of God and to understand the context of our faith in Christ.

I also acknowledge the influence of the President of the Nigerian Baptist Convention, Revered Doctor Israel Adelani Akanji, immediate past Senior Pastor of First Baptist Church, Garki Abuja, Pastor Oluleke Akinola, my dear brother and General Overseer of Upper Room Baptist Church, Lagos, and Revered Gilbert Oghifo, erstwhile Pastor of Central Baptist Church, Ughelli, Delta State. I am greatly indebted to my beloved wife, Pastor (Mrs) Judith Morka, who has walked in step with me since our call to ministry in 1995. I am also grateful to all brothers and sisters with whom I have interacted in the various churches in which I have been privileged to serve.

Godwin E Morka
17ᵗʰ December 2021

ॐ FOREWORD ॐ

The author of the book, "The Lukewarm Church" Pastor Godwin Morka is a Christian with many years of experience and has served as a church worker, teacher, pastor, preacher and counsellor.

These experiences have given him an in-depth knowledge and understanding of the Church of God. As an administrator and researcher in the secular world, he could see the impact the Church of today has made and is making on the outside - the world and market place. The contents of this book are informed by his experience both in the Church and outside the Church.

While Robert Leardon, the author of the popular book, "God's General" considered using lives of persons in the contemporary world to teach lessons on successful and failed ministries, Pastor Morka used situations in the Bible, to show us the state of the current Church and how we can avoid their pitfalls and mistakes. Specifically, the author focused on the following:

- Worldliness and syncretism of Gideon
- Lukewarmness of the Laodicea church
- Materialism and covetousness of Balaam
- The individualistic attitude of many church leaders as represented in the life of Samson. Many church leaders seek their interests instead of the Kingdom's and the church is suffering from this inordinate desire and lust for power, money, and influence.
- Saul's inordinate ambition and disobedience
- And many other personalities as it relates to the situation in the church today.

The author emphasized the loss of the Church's desire and hunger for the things of God - soul winning, bible-based teachings, discipleship, charity, etc. and he made a call for the Church to repent and return to God. A believer belongs to God, we are special and a chosen generation that has been called out and must separate ourselves from the pervasiveness of the world.

In his words, "these qualities will certainly mark Christians out as different; our lives will display the goodness of God – proclaiming the praises and glory of God in our daily living. People will see God's goodness in our lives, and note that we are not living like them, in dread of the systems and values of the world. They will come to us for solutions, and we then point them to the Cross – and the matchless grace of God that sustains us in the midst of a perverse world".

The book "The Lukewarm Church" though focused on the Church entails life's lessons that could be learnt by believers for their own personal growth and walk with God, after all the church is made up of believers. From the lives of the different **individuals examined** in the book, we can glean serious wisdom to help us avoid their mistakes and make progress in our walk with God.

I therefore recommend this book to all serious-minded believers who seek to be on fire for God in this end time as we look forward to the coming of Jesus, our Lord and Saviour.

Shalom.
Pastor Oluleke Akinola
General Overseer
Upper Room Baptist Church, Lagos.

℘ ℞

Jesus had warned His disciples in Matthew 24:12 that because of the increase of wickedness, the love of most would grow cold.

In ***The Lukewarm Church***, Pastor Morka engages the post-covid Church on the dangers inherent in lukewarmness. Taking from the Church in the Book of Revelation (with special emphasis on the Laodicean Church), he draws inspiration from characters in the Bible like Lot, Saul, Ananias and Sapphira and the seven sons of Sceva to call our attention on the dangers of lukewarmness.

If there is a message that the Church needs today, it is the wake-up call from the slumber of lukewarmness.

Pastor Morka therefore gives the clarion call for a return to an uncompromising lifestyle of holiness.

Reverend Tom Takpatore
Acting Senior Pastor, First Baptist Church, Garki-Abuja
20th May 2022

ഊ ൯

This is a beautiful piece, very easy to read, and very apt for today's Christian and Church members alike.

It is a very timely book that would serve to remind older Christians and ministers of the gospel as the basis and focus of their calling, and as well exhort young believers and new entrants into the ministry on particular areas to be cautious about.

I share your view on the present dangerous compromise that the Church and her leaders have fallen into which has led to the Church losing her voice and authority especially in a nation like ours.

The book would serve as a wake-up call to the redeemed who still have the light of God burning in their heart.

Reverend Dr. Alexander Ikechukwu Omosor
Rector, Upper Room Bible College, Lagos

છ ૹ

One of the challenges facing us as a Church is that many congregation members do not read the Bible. Nevertheless, when some of them do, they do not even have the capacity for perfect understanding.

Many have heard about the Old Testament characters like Samson, Joseph, David, Gideon, Jacob and New Testament exemplifications of Churches like the Laodecian Church, etc.

How many Church members, including the preachers, understand how these mentions relate to the current congregation, how much more learn from them? My friend and brother, Godwin Morka has done great justice to this anticipation.

With a quality attribute of eloquent explanation and lucid illumination, he has been able to tweak the ear of the recalcitrant and lukewarm church members.
He has also been able to interpret the Bible for the baby Christians still hooked to milk.

Every Christian will see himself in the book. It is not just apposite to just read it, but to also pass it unto members of the Church with great expectation of evangelism.

If we must be prepared for His second coming, the lukewarm Church must wake up from its deep slumber!

Dr. Bola Adewara
Editor E-life magazine
Presenter, Mentoring Masterclass

ꟿ ꟿ

ꙮ INTRODUCTION ꙮ

THE SEVEN CHURCHES

Revelations 3:14-22

The Book of Revelations Chapters 2 and 3 contain seven letters addressed by the LORD Jesus Christ to each of the seven major churches in Asia Minor, with a description of each church:

Ephesus (Revelations Chapter 2, verses 1 to 7) –

This Church was commended for labouring hard without being discouraged and had separated itself from the evil in its environment.

The Church had exercised the courage to confront those who pretended to be apostles, and rejected their messages.

However, the LORD accused the church of having forsaken its first love (Revelation 2:4). The Church was admonished to return to its original height and practise what it first believed.

Smyrna (Revelations Chapter 2, verses 8 to 11) –

The LORD noted the apparent afflictions and poverty of this Church but assured it that it is indeed rich toward God. The LORD admonished the church to be determined to overcome the adversities that it would surely face with the assurance that it would eventually receive the crown of life

Pergamum (Revelations Chapter 2, verses 12-17) –

Despite being located in the very city where Satan had his throne, that is where Satan lived, this Church remained steadfastly loyal to the Name of the LORD and never renounced their faith, even in the face of martyrdom. The Church was, however, warned to get rid of the licentious teachings and practices of the Nicolaitans - followers of Nicolas, one of the seven deacons (Acts 6:5), who, like Balaam, promoted free love.

Thyatira (Revelation Chapter 2, verses18-29) –

The LORD acknowledged the deeds, love and faith, service and perseverance, as well as the ever-increasing diligence of this Church. However, it had in its midst a seductive prophetess who was corrupting the Church by teaching sexual immorality and eating foods offered to idols. The LORD's promise is that He would severely punish the adulterous woman and her followers if they did not repent but He would spare the rest of the Church.

Sardis (Revelation Chapter3, verses1-6) –

The LORD gave a damning verdict about this Church: it had a reputation of being alive but was actually dead. The Church was advised to fan the embers of the little life left in it, and was assured of severe judgment if it failed, though the few virtuous members of the Church would be rewarded.

Philadelphia (Revelation Chapter 3, verses 7-13) –

It is the only Church that had no blame. The Church had been steadfast in faith, and the LORD assured it of assistance to overcome its adversaries, as evidence of the love of the LORD. It was to hold on to what it had because its reward was sure.

Laodicea (Revelation Chapter 3 verses 14-22) –

The lukewarm and insipid church, neither hot nor cold, and the LORD threatened to spit it out of His mouth. This Church was under the illusion that it was wealthy and self-sufficient, but the LORD said that in reality, it was "wretched, pitiful, poor, blind and naked" (Revelation 3:17). The LORD counselled this Church to seek wealth, adornment and healing from Him, assuring them that His grace was still available.

Some Bible scholars have posited that these letters were specifically addressed to and concerned the seven Churches in Asia Minor; while others like Cyrus Ingerson Scofield, the American Theologian and writer believe that the seven Churches represent seven different eras of the Christian Church from the time of Paul until the return of the LORD Jesus Christ.

According to Scofield, "these messages by their very terms go beyond the local assemblies mentioned," He also posited that the letters prophetically disclosed the spiritual history of the Church. Charles Ryrie states that the seven Churches were actual Churches in John's day, but that they also represented the types and conditions of Churches in all generations.

This book does not intend to join issues with any of these eminent scholars but rather it aims at presenting a picture of today's Church from the prism of some Old Testament and New Testament characters, using the Laodicean Church as our template.

The LORD described the Church in Laodicea as:

- Lukewarm
- Having an illusion of wealth and self-sufficiency
- Wretched
- Pitiful

- Poor
- Blind
- Naked

Each of the characters treated in this book depicted these characteristics in their lives, taking the Grace of God upon their lives for granted. It is my firm view that today's Churches mirror these same characteristics.

It is also my belief that the warning the LORD gave to the Laodicean Church is still valid for our age - ***"I counsel you to buy from Me gold refined in the fire, so that you can become rich; and white clothes to wear, so you can cover your shameful nakedness; and salve to put on your eyes, so you can see."*** (Revelation Chapter 3:18).

We are in the dispensation of Grace, and the Church of Christ seems to be taking this Grace for granted in so many ways. What pertains to the Church also pertains to individual Christians. It is my prayer that we shall see ourselves in the lives of these Bible characters and heed the warning of the LORD Jesus Christ before it is too late!

Godwin E. Morka

1

ഇ LOT ഇ:

CARELESS WITH GOD'S GRACE

The story of Lot is told in the book of Genesis Chapters 12 to Chapter 19. However, he was first introduced in the closing verses of Genesis 11 as the son of Haran, the brother of Abraham. Haran died relatively young and his father, Terah succeeded him, and became responsible for the upbringing of Lot.

It was actually Terah who left Ur of the Chaldees with his son, Abram with his wife Sarai, as well as Lot, his grandson to set out for Canaan. However, their journey ended at a village called Haran, probably so named in memory of Terah's son, the father of Lot. Terah died in Haran at the age of 205 years. Genesis 11:27-32.

It was at Haran that Abram received the call of the LORD to go to a place He would show him, and that he got the promise that he was going to become the father of many nations, though at the age of 75 years, he and his wife Sarai still had no child. Therefore, Abram left Haran with his wife, his nephew Lot, all his wealth and servants, and eventually arrived near Shechem in the land of Canaan.

After the famine in Shechem and a brief sojourn in Egypt, Abram and his household went to dwell in the Negev, at a place between Ai and Bethel, and they settled there. Over time, Lot became so wealthy that the land could no longer support both Abram and Lot's businesses, and quarrels began to break out between his herdsmen and Abram's herdsmen.

As a solution, Abram suggested that he and Lot should move apart; he made Lot an offer to choose which way to go.

Lot took a long look at the fertile plains of the Jordan Valley in the direction of Zoar. The whole area was well watered everywhere, like the garden of the LORD or the beautiful land of Egypt...Lot chose that land for himself - the Jordan Valley to the east of them...Genesis 13:10-11

That was a pivotal point in the relationship between Abram and Lot, and one that revealed the true character of Lot. Thus far, he had enjoyed the vicarious blessings and grace bestowed on Abram as promised by God. He had become very wealthy with lots of servants, sheep, cattle and many tents (Genesis 13:5) but he forgot the source of his wealth. He failed to appreciate that his blessings flowed from God's blessings on Abraham, and that he was enjoying the grace God had bestowed on Abraham.

In Genesis Chapter 14 Lot was taken hostage by a consortium of kings led by King Amraphel of Sinar, who had successfully quelled the rebellion of the kings of Sodom, Gomorrah, Admah, Zeboiim and Bela. Lot was important enough to have become a prisoner of war. An escapee informed Abraham of what had befallen his nephew. Abraham had to mobilise his household army who were able to rescue Lot and other hostages.

Lot had obviously joined the elite of Sodom and Gomorrah. He was at the city gate when the angels that were to destroy Sodom and Gomorrah arrived, and he took them to his house (Genesis 19) while his uncle Abraham was still living in tents. Earlier in the book of Genesis Chapter 18, Abraham laboured in the place of prayer interceding for Lot and his household, and God once again extended Grace to him because of Abraham.

One would have expected Lot to be a holy influence in his adopted city and region. Instead, he had become assimilated into their way of life, but for the Grace of God that kept him somewhat apart. He obviously still had the fear of God and led a religious life. However, he gave out his daughters in marriage to men of the city who did not fear or reverence the God of Abraham.

After getting the message of God through the angels, he tried, but could not convince his married daughters and their husbands to flee with him. Only his wife and his two virgin daughters agreed to leave the city with him, even though reluctantly.

Lot had the Grace of experiencing God at work in the life of his uncle, Abraham. Nevertheless, his love for the good things of life caused him to choose the part of the land he considered verdant and productive.

He also lived it up in his adopted cities and mixed up with them, rather than standing out as a witness to the true God. He never achieved the purpose for which God sent him to Sodom and Gomorrah. He wasted the Grace of God upon his life and ended up with an error that caused so much distress to Abraham's descendants later in history.

(Lot) wasted the Grace of God upon his life and ended up with an error that caused so much distress to Abraham's descendants later in history.

He had an incestuous relationship with his two daughters that led to the birth of Ammon and Moab, the progenitors of the worst enemies of the descendants of Abraham. Lot was lukewarm, careless, had an illusion of wellbeing, but ended up wretched and pitiful, like the Laodicean Church, (Revelations 3:15-17).

The LORD Jesus Christ left His Church in the world and He returned to Heaven so that the Church might be the salt and light of the earth. He said that though we are in the world, we are not of the world, (John 17:16).

However, just like Lot, the Church has begun to enjoy the perquisites of life on earth - influence, material prosperity, and oneness with the world. The Church has increasingly become an organisation governed by the laws of man, rather than the spiritual organism that depends for its growth on the nourishment of the word of God and the Power of the Holy Spirit.

Abraham laboured in the place of prayer interceding for Lot and his household, and God once again extended Grace to him because of Abraham.

Church leaders now sit in the gates with the rulers of this world, and have become so indistinguishable from their worldly counterparts that when they try to admonish holiness, the people are both surprised and flabbergasted.

Lot struggled to convince even his married daughters and their husbands to flee Sodom and Gomorrah. What a tragic realisation it must have been for him, to know that he had not led by example, and had not modelled his life according to the faith of Abraham!

The way many Church leaders carry on and scramble for the lucre of this world, you would hardly believe that they have the Spirit of Christ in them. They preach and teach the systems of this world, couched in biblical language. So much 'preaching' but no power, except such as comes by man's efforts, connections and knowledge.

In times of national crises, world leaders ought to turn to the Church for spiritual guidance and superior wisdom: to lead prayers for God's mercy and intervention.

However, increasingly, government leaders hardly consider the Church because most Church leaders have lost their moral authority. How can someone who has received bribes from politicians, political office holders or who has indulged in dirty deals turn round, preach holiness, and want to speak as God's oracle?

"Son of man, these men have set up idols in their hearts,

And put before them that which causes

Them to stumble into iniquity.

Should I let Myself be inquired of at all by them?" (Ezekiel 14:3)

During the Coronavirus (Covid-19) global pandemic, Churches were among the first public places causally closed down all around the world. Not even the Pope could offer any solution or reason why the Vatican, a so-called sovereign nation should not be shuttered.

More disasters will come to the world. Judgment Day is fast approaching and many souls are bound for hell. The Church, which should be sounding the alarm, is too busy with noisy conventions, puerile fellowships and barren worship services that cater to the egos and delusions of men, rather than to the spiritual needs of the people and the exultation of the Name of Jesus.

> *"I hate all your show and pretence -*
>
> *The hypocrisy of your religious festivals*
>
> *And solemn assemblies"* (Amos 5:21) NLT
>
> *"I hate, I despise your feast days,*
>
> *And I do not savour your sacred assemblies"*

(Amos 5:21) NKJV

The Post-Covid-19 era should steer the Church back to its first love and to the Rock from which it was hewn. The stark demonstration of the irrelevance of the Church during the pandemic should serve as a wake-up call to all discerning Christians.

Let us not be like Lot who, though he escaped disaster, suffered irreparable losses caused indelible pains.

2

ഇ BALAAM ര:

SEEKING GOD'S PERMISSIVE WILL

The story of Balaam occupies three chapters of the book of Numbers: Chapter 22, Chapter 24, and with the consequences of his perfidy depicted in Chapter 25. He was mentioned in seven books of the Bible.

The name **Balaam** means 'destroyer of the people.' He was a pagan seer, the son of Beor from the town of Pethor. He was not an Israelite, and therefore not one of God's chosen people.

Joshua Chapter 13:22 describes Balaam as a **diviner,** who used magic to tell the future. This ability was based on witchcraft, not on the unction of the Holy Spirit.

Balaam was apparently quite famous in Mesopotamia because he lived quite some distance from King Balak the Moabite who sent for his help.

According to Vijay Thangiah, who retired in 2016 as National Director of Youth for Christ, after 40 years of service, "Balaam was a mercenary prophet of the worst kind. He was famous, self-willed, double-minded, eloquent, presumptuous and an evil counsellor."

Balaam was an enigmatic character. Though he was a sorcerer, he knew about the God of Israel, and referred to Him by His Covenant Name, Jehovah. He was a man who knew a great deal of truth about God but lived a life based on occultism. He never said anything wrong, but he never did anything right. His mouth was filled with things of the Spirit, but his heart was filled with the things of the flesh.

The first time the nobles of Moab came to Balaam, God expressly instructed Him what to do – ***"Do not go with them. You are not to curse these people, for they have been blessed!"*** (Numbers 22:12, NLT).

Every true prophet of God knows the importance of obeying God instinctively. However, Balaam, being a mercenary fortune-teller, refused to take God's word as final. Instead, in sending the Moabite princes back, he left room for further 'negotiations' by telling them, ***"Jehovah refuses to give me leave to go with you"*** (Numbers 22:13, DARBY).

King Balak interpreted Balaam's refusal to come, to mean that he needed a bigger fee. Therefore, he sent higher-level officials with a caveat that he would promote Balaam to any position of honour and pay whatever it would take Balaam to curse Israel for him.

In response, Balaam went into a superficial pontification - ***"Even if Balak were to give me his palace filled with silver and gold, I would be powerless to do anything against the will of the LORD my God."*** (Numbers 22:18)

At this point, Balaam ticked all the boxes concerning knowledge of God's will and his duty to obey God. However, he betrayed the contents of his heart in the next sentence: ***"But stay here one more night, and I will see if the LORD has anything else to say to me."*** (Number 22:19)

That was the crux of Balaam's religion - dissatisfaction with God's direct instructions, and seeking to make God change His mind and allowing something less than His perfect will.

Even though he disavowed Balak's tempting promises, his heart obviously yearned for them. In addition, of course, he 'heard' what he wanted to hear from the LORD, that he should now go with the Moabite envoys but to speak only what the LORD would instruct.

Unfortunately, the religion of Balaam has become the religion of many of today's Christians. We seek God's second opinion on His express commands in the Bible or the clear instructions of the Holy Spirit, twist the word of God, or put God to puerile tests aimed at following our minds but attributing it to **'God's permissive will'.**

Like Balaam, we delude ourselves that we are spiritual enough to know where to draw the line, that we would remain 'obedient' to God even in our waywardness. Like Balaam, we also quote ***"God is not a man that He should lie, nor the son of man that He should repent..."*** (Numbers 23:19, KJV).

Hypocrites quote the Bible to deceive and twist it to cover their evil ways. The Word of God stands sure and it is not subject to revision or to a 'new edition'.

Every true prophet of God knows the importance of obeying God instinctively

What was true in the beginning is still true today. Like the Church of Laodicea, the modern Church is neither hot nor cold (Revelations 3: 15) because we obey the word of God in the breach.

We go searching the Bible for verses we can take out of context to justify our wilfulness and disobedience, our worldliness and desire for filthy lucre.

How long can the church hope to retain the love and mercy of God when we have no stomach for the Biblical truth, or mouth the scriptures without attempting to put them into practice?

The LORD warned the Laodicean Church that He would 'spew' it out of His mouth; can the modern church expect to escape this inevitable judgment?

To demonstrate the inerrancy of His word, and that Balaam never got His permission, God sent an angel to stop Balaam on his ill-fated mission. Balaam was so blinded by the allure of the reward he was expecting from Balak that he did not see the angel even though his donkey could see him. (Numbers 22:23-34).

God demonstrated His love for His children, Israel, by intervening to make sure that Balaam blessed rather than curse them. God could have annulled whatever curse Balaam could have placed on the Israelites, or He could have decided to kill Balaam in the process.

Like Balaam, we delude ourselves that we are spiritual enough to know where to draw the line

Nevertheless, He allowed the story to play out that way to exhibit His overwhelming Grace upon His children in the midst of so much evil and wickedness in the world in which we live.

On arrival in Beor, Balak took Balaam to many choice sites and vantage positions from which to curse Israel, because he knew that Balaam was a very covetous man.

Balaam knew God's mind concerning this mission because God told him expressly the first time he asked. Rather than obey God, he allowed his greed to becloud his sense of propriety.

Many may argue that Balaam was not an Israelite and not a prophet of God like Moses; but people believed that he was a prophet, and he actually did hear from God.

Balaam's inordinate greed led him to give a counsel that eventually led to the contamination of the children of Israel through sexual impurity, and the death of many.

Unfortunately, many pastors and men of God in our time are exactly like Balaam, and are in the ministry for personal gain and profit.

They have a gift of the garb, are versed in the affairs of this world, and therefore exhibit high-sounding words and hints of esoteric knowledge and insight in order to deceive their gullible followers.

> We go searching the Bible for verses we can take out of context to justify our wilfulness and disobedience, our worldliness and desire for filthy lucre.

Through their puerile preaching, mixed with biblical allusions, the modern-day Balaams seek to reinterpret the mind of God for their followers. Fear them when you hear terms like "God's permissive will", "Hyper-grace", "my prophetic throne room" and other such inanities.

The Balaams of our time occupy the majority of church pulpits, but I am convinced that out of each of those congregations, God will soon raise 'donkeys' who will proclaim the mind of God and save true seekers of God from perdition.

3

ஃ GIDEON ஆ:

FROM GRACE TO GRASS

The story of Gideon is a classic story of someone rising from grass to Grace by the divine election of God. Indeed, Judges Chapter 6, verse1 to Chapter 8, verse 21 reads like a film script, in which a literal nobody suddenly makes good and becomes the ruler of all that he sees.

After the death of Deborah, the children of Israel went back to their cycle of sin and repentance. Judges Chapter 6, verses 1 to 4 (NKJV) say:

"Then the children did evil in the sight of the LORD. So the LORD delivered them into the hand of Midian for seven years.

and the hand of Midian prevailed against Israel.

Because of the Midianites, the children of Israel made for themselves the dens, the caves, and the strongholds which are in the mountains.

So it was, whenever Israel had sown, Midianites would come up; also Amalekites and the people of the East would come up against them.

Then they would encamp against them and destroy the produce of the earth as far as Gaza, and leave no sustenance for Israel, neither sheep nor ox nor donkey."

When the children of Israel cried out to the LORD, He sent a prophet to reassure them of His abiding love, while rebuking their idolatrous ways.

It was in this scenario that the Angel of the LORD appeared to Gideon (one of the Theophanies of Christ) while he was threshing wheat in a winepress in order to hide it from the Midianites (Judges 6, verse 11).

The Angel of the LORD addressed Gideon as, **'You mighty man of valour!'** whereas he was obviously a cowering coward who also recognised his severe limitations – from the weakest clan in Manasseh, and the least in his father's house.

The LORD commissioned him to **'Go in this might of yours, and you shall save Israel from the hand of the Midianites'** Judges 6, verse 14.

In other words, God did not give Gideon a special training, nor did He require any proof of prowess from Gideon. God was saying to him, yes you are the smallest man from the smallest family and the smallest clan, but in your weakness and inability, I will get victory for Israel!

Right from the outset, it was clear that Gideon was simply an instrument God wanted to use to defeat the Midianites and that it was not about Gideon's military capabilities or bravery.

Gideon himself recognised this and put up several tests to be sure that God would follow through and use him mightily as promised. God's Grace on Gideon's life was overwhelming as demonstrated in the string of victories he had over much stronger enemy-armies.

The first demonstration of this grace was right in his father's house. His father, Joash, was a devotee of Baal,

The Angel of the LORD addressed Gideon as, **'You mighty man of valour!'** whereas he was obviously a cowering coward…

and had built an altar to Baal along with an Asherah pole in his compound.

The LORD instructed Gideon to pull down the shrines of Baal, and erect an altar to the God of Israel, and then to sacrifice a bull on it. Buoyed by the boldness God had instilled in him, Gideon did as the LORD had instructed, even though he did it at night out when everyone else was asleep.

By the next morning, Baal's adherents had discovered what Gideon had done and demanded that Joash should bring him out to be killed for the sacrilege he had committed against their god.

Joash who had obviously noticed something different about his son, Gideon, gave the town folks a classic answer: if Baal is a god, let him fight for himself!

After all, the God of Israel never needed anyone to fight for Him! Nobody could argue against that, and Gideon was renamed Jerubbaal – let Baal defend himself!

Soon, the trilogy of enemies – Midian, Amalek and the people of the East – coalesced against Israel. Gideon

God was saying to him, yes you are the smallest man from the smallest family and the smallest clan, but in your weakness and inability, I will get victory for Israel!

summoned the valiant men of Israel from Manasseh, Asher, Zebulun and Naphtali. To further demonstrate his lack of confidence in his own abilities, Gideon further put God through the test of the fleece (Judges 6, verses 36 to 40).

Gideon assembled an army of 32,000 men, but God wanted to demonstrate to him that he was only going to win because of God's mighty grace with him.

God trimmed Gideon's army to a mere 300 men, who eventually did not raise a sword, but rather blew rams' horns and broke clay jars to defeat the mighty Midianite army. God also enabled him to kill the two Midianite kings, and to destroy Succoth and Peniel with his rag-tag army.

Up to this point, Gideon's humility and recognition of the grace of God upon his life was very apparent. Even after his string of victories, when Israel wanted to establish a kingly lineage through him, Gideon refused, and rather told the people that the God of Israel would be their King.

Right from the outset, it was clear that Gideon was simply an instrument God wanted to use to defeat the Midianites and that it was not about Gideon's military capabilities or bravery

However, he asked each of them to contribute a gold earring from the spoils of war, which they all gladly did.

The gold weighed 19.3 kilogrammes and he made it into a golden ephod, the likeness of a priestly robe, which he installed in his hometown, Ophrah. Israelites soon began to worship this image, and it became a snare for Gideon and his family.

"For rebellion is as the sin of witchcraft,

And stubbornness is as iniquity and idolatry…" 1 Samuel Chapter 15, verse 23

The story of Gideon is the story of today's Church. Many pastors have been raised by God out of total obscurity to places of prominence in His Kingdom on earth.

God has used them to redeem many from satanic oppressions, from disease and darkness; and has used them to do exploits and miracles; to speak with authority, and to gain respect and honour among men.

God trimmed Gideon's army to a mere 300 men, who eventually did not raise a sword, but rather blew rams' horns and broke clay jars to defeat the mighty Midianite army.

They start out full of humility, acknowledging the Grace of God upon their lives, and calling on God publicly to help them.

However, as the years pass, they get used to being idolised. They gradually become worldly and crave human adulation and affirmation. They pander to those in authority for positions and filthy lucre, and become enmeshed in politics. While still espousing the Gospel and the suzerainty of Heaven, such pastors preach other gospels – prosperity, mantles, dangerous prayers, syncretism, positive thinking, inordinate ambition, self-will and self-empowerment, self-centredness, motivational talks and other such practices.

These teachings derail and weaken the faith of many of their followers just as Gideon remained a respectable leader and man of God, but allowed his followers to worship the golden ephod of Ophrah.

That is why the Church has lost its voice and relevance in our times. Political leaders take the views espoused by religious leaders, including Christian leaders, for granted.

During the 2020 Covid-19 Pandemic, churches were among the public places that governments around the world shut down right at the outset, with little or no consultation with church leaders.

The irony is that the Presidents, Prime Ministers and Governors who first imposed the shuttering of church doors were mostly Christians, and the people that applauded this move most, were Christians.

Those church leaders who kicked against the shutdown of churches, especially in Nigeria, spoke with so much venom against the government of the day that the public received their complaints mostly as partisan bellyaching.

There was hardly any constructive engagement with government at State or Federal levels by the Christian community until much later.

The Church in Nigeria also has to contend with the spirit of ecumenism and inter-faith rapprochements, which has progressively blurred the distinction between Christianity and other religious practices.

The result is that the civic authorities often place Christianity on the same or even lower pedestals with other religions.

No matter how much Christian leaders assure orderliness and obedience to health guidelines during

However, as the years pass, the pastors get used to being idolised. They gradually become worldly and crave human adulation and affirmation.

Church services, they cannot get any considerations other than what applies to mosques, for example, which are notorious for rowdy gatherings even in the midst of grave threats to public health posed by Covid-19.

The Church is supposedg to be the light and salt of the earth, but worldliness, compromise, syncretism, materialism and relativism have conspired to becloud the glory of the church. However, as the LORD assures: *'...the gates of hell shall not prevail'* against the church, Matthew 16, verse 18).

4

৪ SAMSON ৪:

ABUSE OF GRACE

Samson is one of the tragic heroes of the Bible (Judges Chapters 13 to 16). He was from Zorah, of the family of the Danites. His father's name was Manoah, and his wife was barren because she had not conceived after many years of marriage.

The Angel of the LORD appeared to Samson's mother on a fateful day, and announced that she was going to conceive and bear a son who would *'begin to deliver Israel out of the hand of the Philistines'* (Judges Chapter 13, verses 3 to 5).

Samson was to be a Nazirite to God from the womb, and no razor should come upon his head. His mother was also to abstain from wine and anything unclean. Samson's mother recognised that she had experienced a special visitation from God, because in reporting to her husband, she said, ***"A Man of God came to me, and His countenance was like the countenance of the Angel of God, very awesome..."*** (Judges Chapter 13, verse 6).

Theologians generally agree that this was one of the Theophanies of Christ or Christophanies – when Christ appeared in visible form in the Old Testament, before His physical manifestation in the New Testament, usually recognised by the term, 'The Angel of the LORD'.

The main distinguishing factor between The Angel of the LORD and other angels is that He accepted the worship and sacrifices of men, while the ordinary angels would not.

> Samson was to be a Nazirite to God from the womb

God kept His promises regarding Samson, and gave him supernatural strength with which he would subdue the Philistines. (Judges Chapter 13, verse 24)

Unfortunately, the first adult action credited to Samson was that on his visit to Timnah, he became besotted with a Philistine woman, and demanded that his parents 'get her' for him as his wife.

Of course, this set off alarm bells for his parents who admonished him to get a wife from among the Israelites. However, Samson insisted that it was the Philistine woman or nothing.

Even though the Bible notes that this was God's design, it might be difficult to understand why God would contradict His own instructions to the Israelites (Deuteronomy Chapter 7, verse 1 to 4), even though there have been exemptions.

However, Samson's action should be viewed in the context that God still used Samson's wilful disobedience to accomplish His purpose.

Apart from Rahab and Ruth who proclaimed faith in the God of Israel, many of the other cross-cultural marriages brought much grief to the nation of Israel.

Unfortunately, the first adult action credited to Samson was that on his visit to Timnah, he became besotted with a Philistine woman,

Against their better judgement, the parents of Samson accompanied him to Timnah, and on the way, as they passed through the vineyards of the Philistines, a lion suddenly jumped out to attack them. Samson tore the lion in pieces through divine assistance, but did not tell the parents what he had done.

On the day they went back for the marriage feast, Samson went to look at the carcass of the lion he had killed and found a swarm of bees on it. He scooped honey from the beehive and ate it; he also gave his parents some of it without telling them the source.

During the seven-day feast, Samson gave a riddle to his hosts, promising them 30 linen garments and 30 sets of clothes if they succeeded in solving the riddle. The riddle had to do with his getting sweet honey out of the carcass of a strong lion.

For seven days and nights, Samson's bride pestered him at the instigation of her fellow Philistines. Finally, on the seventh day, he told her the answer, which she promptly relayed to her sponsors. Samson was infuriated, went out to kill 30 Philistines, and took their clothing to fulfil his vow. He left his wife behind in anger and returned to his home.

A few months later, he went back to get his wife from his parents-in-law, but they had given her out in marriage to his best man!

This incensed Samson the more, and he set out to destroy the vineyards and the grain farms of the Philistines by tying flaming torches to the tails of 150 pairs of foxes.

Instead of learning from his debacle with his Philistine wife, Samson soon fell for a loose Philistine woman called Delilah, who beguiled him until he disclosed the source of his superhuman powers, leading ultimately to his death.

Samson is often rightly hailed as a hero of faith (Hebrews Chapter 11, verses 32 and 33), because of his great exploits even at the point of death (Judges Chapter 16, verses 1 to 3 and 28 to 30).

Just imagine what greater things Samson could have achieved if he had followed God's plans for his life faithfully.

What kind of hero was Samson when his own people betrayed him to the Philistines? After the Philistines confronted the armies of Judah because of Samson (Judges Chapter 15, verse 9), the people of Judah decided to give in to their demands and hand over Samson.

Three thousand of his own people ostensibly politely asked Samson for permission to capture him and turn him over to the Philistines. He agreed with them on the condition that they would not kill him by themselves. He then allowed them to tie him up and deliver him to their enemies. However, he literally became a wrecking ball in the land of the Philistines, killing one thousand of them with the jawbone of an ass.

Samson was consecrated for a special purpose by God. The locks of hair on his head were a symbol of that consecration. When Samson fell to the allurements of Delilah, and the locks of hair were cut, he lost his strength, not because of the locks of hair, but because of the assault on his consecration.

According to Charles Haddon (CH) Spurgeon –Baptist preacher dubbed 'The Prince of Preachers' – (Sermon No 224, Sabbath Morning, 21st November 1858), "While his hair was untouched, he was a consecrated man; as soon as that was cut away, he was no longer perfectly consecrated, and then his strength departed from him."

Once Samson had become weak, he became an object of ridicule amongst the Philistines he once terrorised. Gaza, the city whose massive gates he had earlier pulled up and carried on his shoulders, became his prison. His eyes were gouged out, and he was subjected to the cruellest of treatments, and taunted by his captors.

> (Samson) lost his strength, not because of the locks of hair, but because of the assault on his consecration.

This pathetic picture is a stark warning to all Christians that we are consecrated by God to do His will but when we are negligent or abusive of our consecration, we become vulnerable to falling into the torments of the enemy – Satan the devil.

The symbol of our anointing is not outward like Samson's hair locks, but the awesome Presence of the

Holy Spirit in our hearts. He is our Guide, or Barometer, our Teacher and our Helper or Paraclete.

We must be careful not to abuse this precious Gift of God – Grace unsearchable! Samson abused the grace of God upon his life.

He used his strength to pursue parochial causes, not the collective aspiration of the children of Israel. There is no record that he ever mustered an army like his predecessors nor addressed any council of elders to articulate a plan or share God's messages for His people.

Because he was mostly fighting his personal battles, his people never fully appreciated his heroics; and he never really subdued the Philistines, but was merely a terrible irritant to them. No wonder, the people of Judah were willing to hand over their champion to the Philistines!

The Church in Samson

The Church was founded on the LORDSHIP and Deity of Christ (Matthew Chapter 16, verses 16 to 19). On the day of Pentecost, the LORD breathed life into the Church

The symbol of our anointing is not outward like Samson's hair locks, but the awesome Presence of the Holy Spirit in our hearts. He is our Guide, or Barometer, our Teacher and our Helper or Paraclete.

by sending the Holy Spirit upon the disciples who had gathered in the Upper Room. He sent them as witnesses to Him to every part of the world.

That is the sole purpose of the Church: to represent Christ, to model Him, and to turn the world to Christ.

In His High Priestly prayer, Jesus emphasised that though we are in the world, we are not part of the world (John Chapter 17, verses 14 to 20). If we are to model Christ, we are expected to mirror His precepts, His values and His character; these can be discerned and seen from His ministry.

Right at the beginning of His earthly Ministry, the LORD was subjected to temptation by Satan (Matthew Chapter 4, verses 1 to 11). Satan presented all the glory of the world to Him, and the opportunities for power, profit and influence, but the LORD spurned all of Satan's allurements and emphasised the supremacy and sufficiency of the Word of God.

The Apostle Paul underlined our separation from the world in Romans Chapter 12, verses 1 to 2 (KJV):

"I beseech you therefore, brethren, by the mercies of God, that you present your bodies a living sacrifice, holy, acceptable unto God, which is your reasonable service.

"And be ye not conformed to this world: but be ye transformed by the renewing of your mind that ye

may prove what is that good, and acceptable and perfect will of God."

The Apostle John echoed the same admonition in 1John Chapter 2, verses 15 to 16 (KJV):

"Love not the world, neither the things that are in the world. If any man love the world, the love of the Father is not in Him.

"For all that is in the world, the lust of the flesh, and the lust of the eyes, and the pride of life, is not of the Father, but is of the world."

This attitude to the world made the Jews to describe the early Christians as people who had 'turned the world upside down' (Acts Chapter 17, verse 6). Can this be said of today's Christians, or to any extent, Christians who succeeded the Apostolic Fathers?

We must be careful not to abuse this precious Gift of God – Grace unsearchable!

Like Samson, the Church is a product of pure Grace, founded for the clear purpose of taking the world for Christ. Just like Samson, the Church has not fulfilled that purpose, but has ventured into the world to try to appropriate *'the things that are in the world'* - power, profit and influence.

The Church has aspired for political leadership all through the centuries, and this thirst continues in the partisan bent of many church leaders and their desire for political appointments and other largesse from governments around the world. *'Get her for me,'* Samson lustfully demanded; that is how so many Christian leaders lust after worldly power.

The Church has also aggressively pursued the acquisition of wealth and properties since the time of Emperor Constantine.

According to churchandstate.org.uk, 'Catholic priests are expected to make a vow of poverty, so it is ironic that the Church is actually the richest religion in the world. The Catholic Church owns some of the greatest art works ever made. It also has vast gold deposits and billions of dollars in assets.' This is apart from owning some of the best prime properties around the world.

> *'Get her for me,'* Samson lustfully demanded; that is how so many Christian leaders lust after worldly power.

The Anglican Church or the Church of England used to be the biggest landowner in Great Britain. It sold off most of the land to build up an investment portfolio of $6.7 Billion that earns more than $255 million each year, according to the same source. The same can be said of virtually all the other church denominations.

Perhaps, the greatest evidence of the Samson spirit is the shameless desire of many church leaders to become celebrities and superstars.

Some televangelists and some Pentecostals want to be adored like film stars; many preachers relish in the acquisition of private jets, and live the most lavish lifestyles.

Like Samson, they have found their Delilah, and abuse the grace of God upon their lives to please the world system. No wonder the Bible refers to the world system as Babylon. ***'Mystery, Babylon the great, the mother of harlots and of the abomination of the earth.'*** (Revelation Chapter 17, verse 5 NKJV)

Of course, the Bible makes it clear that at the end of it all, the Church will survive the world system, but will it be the triumph of a deformed and lumbering giant, like Samson?.

5

℘ KING SAUL ℃:

TAKING LITTLE THINGS FOR GRANTED
(1 SAMUEL CHAPTERS 9 TO 31)

Saul was a man found by Grace! He literally came out of the blue to become Israel's first king. He came on the scene at the point the Israelites demanded a king so they would be 'like other nations' around them. They were used to judges who led them to war, unlike Samuel who was more of a spiritual guide and conscience of the nation.

During his judgeship, Israel did not need to go to war. When the Philistines tried to attack Israel, God Himself fought for them after Samuel had asked the Israelites to fast and pray, and Samuel had interceded on their behalf. Their enemies were subdued by the direct intervention of God. (1Samuel Chapter 7, verses 1 to 15).

Chapter 8 of First Samuel was pivotal in the relationship between Samuel and Israel. The Israelites indicted Samuel's two sons, Joel and Abijah of *'dishonest gain, bribery and perversion of justice'* (1 Samuel Chapter 8, verse 3). The elders therefore approached Samuel to *'make us a king to judge us like all the nations'* (1Samuel Chapter 8, verse 5).

Samuel was very disappointed with this demand, and expressed his indignation. He warned them of the consequences of their demand, but the people insisted that they needed a king! Samuel took the problem before God, and the LORD asked him to accede to their request.

Their enemies were subdued by the direct intervention of God

This was the scenario when Kish the Benjaminite sent his son, Saul, to go search for his lost donkeys. Saul was described as very tall and handsome.

"There was not a more handsome person than he among the children of Israel, from his shoulders upward he was taller than any of the people" (1 Samuel Chapter 9, verse 2).

After days of fruitless search, Saul suggested to his servant that they return home because his father might have become worried about their safety (1Samuel Chapter 9, verse 6). The servant then further suggested that they consult, in that city, *'a man of God, and he is an honourable man'*

Samuel's reputation as a seer and one who had the ears of God, preceded him, and soon, Saul was face to face with the great man.

Earlier, the LORD had indicated to Samuel that he would meet the chosen one to be king, the next day; and when Saul came close, God pointed him out to Samuel, who then invited Saul to join him to the high place, to eat the feast of sacrifice with him. He also assured him that his father's donkeys had been found.

> (Samuel) warned them of the consequences of their demand, but the people insisted…

That was how Saul encountered his fate as future king of Israel. By the next day, while on his way back home, Samuel anointed him first king of Israel.

A few character traits emerge from this introduction to King Saul:

i. In all the Biblical description of his qualities, there was no mention of his character - just that he was very tall and handsome. To be king would naturally require certain qualities.

ii. Saul's spiritual qualities were never mentioned – was he God-fearing? Did he pray consistently? Was he a notable worshipper of God? Indeed one might argue that he was spiritually shortsighted, because despite a clear direction and description of Samuel, when he came near the man of God, he asked him about how to meet the seer! So close to such a personality and be so undiscerning!

iii. We could see a seeming humility when Samuel first told him he had been favoured by God.

> ***"Saul answered and said, 'Am I not a Benjaminite, of the smallest of tribes in Israel, and my family the least of all the families of the tribe of Benjamin? Why then do you speak like this to me?'"*** (1Samuel Chapter 9, verse 21).

Whether this was true humility or just being politically correct, is left for further discussion.

In 1Samuel Chapters 10 to 12, God's special grace on Saul became manifest immediately he was anointed. Samuel gave him a series of spiritual markers culminating in his being publicly anointed king in Mizpeh. Saul embarked on his new role with a lot of zeal and dedication, starting with the rescue of Jabesh Gilead from the Ammonites.

However, his lack of discernment and spiritual sensitivity became manifest early in his reign when, under pressure from his officials, Saul proceeded to offer the burnt offering at Gilgal when Samuel did not turn up on as promised after seven days. (1Samuel Chapter 13, verses 7 to 9).

As soon as he had finished the sacrifice, Samuel arrived, and Saul gave what would become his standard excuse for his abhorrent behaviour:

"I saw my men scattering from me, and you did not arrive when you said you would, and the Philistines are at Micmash ready for battle. So, I said, 'The Philistines are ready to march against us at Gilgal, and I have not even asked for the LORD's help!' So I felt compelled to offer the burnt offering myself before you came." (1Samuel Chapter 13, verses 11b to 12 NLT).

However, (Saul's) lack of discernment and spiritual sensitivity became manifest early in his reign

Unfortunately, this excuse did not cut any ice with the Prophet Samuel who immediately rebuked Saul and pronounced an end to his dynasty.

Samuel emphasised to Saul the importance of being obedient to the exact commands of God. Unfortunately, Saul was not a man of faith!

The same scenario played itself out in 1Samuel Chapter 15 in Gilgal when Samuel gave Saul express instructions concerning the rules of engagement in Israel's battle with the Amalekites.

Samuel started by reminding Saul that he was the one God had sent to anoint him king over Israel, and admonished him to listen to the message from the LORD:

"I will punish the Amalekites for what they did to Israel when they waylaid them, as they came up from Egypt. Now go, attack the Amalekites and totally destroy everything that belongs to them. Do not spare them; put to death men and women, children and infants, cattle and sheep, camels and donkeys" (1Samuel Chapter 15, verses 2 to 3 NIV).

Saul gave what would become his standard excuse for his abhorrent behaviour

Despite this clear instruction, 1Samuel Chapter 15, verse 9 (NIV) records that:

"But Saul and the army spared (King) Agag and the best of the sheep and cattle, the fat calves and lambs and everything that was good. These they were

unwilling to destroy completely, but everything that was despised and weak they totally destroyed."

When Samuel confronted Saul after the expedition, he quickly declared that he had carried out the LORD's instructions 1Samuel Chapter 15, verse 13. Of course, Samuel already knew what he had done, and thereafter pronounced the death knell on Saul's kingship:

"Does the LORD delight in burnt offerings and sacrifices as much as in obeying the voice of the LORD? To obey is better than sacrifice, and to heed is better than the fat of rams. For rebellion is like the sin of divination and arrogance like the evil of idolatry. Because you have rejected the word of the LORD, He has rejected you as king" (1 Samuel Chapter 15, verses 22 to 23, NIV).

In Saul, we see some characteristics of today's Church:

- Product of God's pure Grace
- Called to be kings under God.

We are privileged to receive instructions from the LORD, but more often than not, we choose to do things our way. We wrongly believe that God will understand and forgive us every time we disobey His commands.

For us Christians, the implication of disobeying God is that we truly do not love Him. In John 15:10, the LORD states that our obedience to His commands is proof of our love for Him.

Saul did not understand the full implication of his disobedience; he probably thought it was a strange instruction, seeing that his soldiers were normally allowed to keep loot from the battlefield.

Saul cared more about the sentiments of his soldiers than the word of God, because just like after the first act of disobedience at Gilgal, he once again, blamed the soldiers (1Samuel Chapter 15, verse 21).

Unfortunately for Saul, it was not business as usual. God had a very important reason for telling him to wipe out the Amalekites, which He was not obliged to disclose to Saul. All that was expected of him was complete obedience.

For us Christians, the implication of disobeying God is that we truly do not love Him.

Fast forward 550 years later, the book of Esther Chapter 2, verses 5 to 6 record:

"Now there was in the Citadel of Susa a Jew of the tribe of Benjamin, named Mordecai son of Jair, the son of Shimei, the son of Kish, who had been carried into exile from Jerusalem by Nebuchadnezzar king of Babylon, among those taken captive with Jehoiachin, King of Judah."

According to Professor Marc Zvi Brettler in his article, *'Megallit Esther: Reversing the Legacy of King Saul'* published in Torah.com,

"Targum Sheni, an expansive midrashic translation of the megillah charts Mordecai's lineage directly to Saul, thus: 'Mordecai, son of Yair, son of Shimei, son of Shemida, son of Ba'ána, son of Ella, son of Micah, son of Mephiboshet, son of Jonathan, son of Saul, son of Kish.'

Professor Brettler goes on to posit that "It is likely that Shimei mentioned here is meant to recall the Benjaminite character in 2Samuel Chapter 16, verses 5 to 8, who had cursed David as he fled Jerusalem during Absalom's rebellion."

Saul cared more about the sentiments of his soldiers than the word of God

According to Brettler, Shimei was mentioned so close to Mordecai even though he must have been a distant ancestor, because he cursed David, but the King had mercy on him and did not have him killed since he must have discerned spiritually, that Mordecai and Esther, through whose hands Israel would be saved, would descend from him.

At this point, we must introduce Haman, the archenemy of the Israelites. The Book of Esther Chapter 3, verse 1 (NIV) states:

"After these events King Xerxes honoured Haman, son of Hammedatha, the Agagite, elevating him and giving him a seat of honour higher than all the other nobles."

This brings us full circle to the drama that started in 1Samuel Chapter 15, and the reason for God's scorched-earth stance towards the Amalekites. Saul's task was to avert this future calamity, but he lacked the spiritual discernment to understand the import of God's instruction. Because of his negligence and disobedience, the Jewish nation was brought to the brink of extinction by a representative of their ancient enemies – Amalekites.

> (Saul) lacked the spiritual discernment to understand the import of God's instruction

Haman was a 16-generation descendant of King Agag, who Saul had refused to kill, along with some or all of the royal family, one of whom was the ancestor of Haman. Almost 600 years later, the deep animosity of the Amalekites, now represented by the Agagites, welled up in Haman, and he sought to use his privileged position to exterminate the Jews.

God's poetic justice and the sanctity of His word came into play here by His ensuring that a descendant of Saul completed the task he had failed to accomplish - the extermination of the Amalekites (Esther Chapter 9, verses 1 to 17).

Verse 10 solemnly notes that after killing the Agagites, including the 10 sons of Haman, *'but they did not lay their hands on the plunder'*. They must have been aware of the historical implication of what they were doing, and ensured that they reversed the disobedience of Saul!

"So shall my word be that goes forth from My mouth; it shall not return to Me void, but it shall accomplish what I please, and it shall prosper in the thing which I sent it" (Isaiah Chapter 55, verse 11).

Perhaps if Saul had understood the full ramifications of the task, he might have behaved differently. God does not always give us the full picture but gives us instructions that He expects us to obey.

Many Christians, like King Saul, take the things of God for granted, thereby falling into big problems.

To obey is better than sacrifice and to heed is better than the fat of rams.

The Bible is full of examples of little things that turned out to have grave consequences. Most times negligence arises out of undue familiarity with the things of God, or on experiences.

God does not always do things the same way He did them before. His instructions are always specific for a purpose. It is not up to us to rationalise or question why God is asking us to do things in certain ways. Our duty is simply to obey.

The Church in Laodicea was so self-assured that it took God's grace for granted:

"You say, 'I am rich; I have acquired wealth and do not need a thing. But you do not realise that you are wretched, pitiful, poor, blind, and naked." (Revelation Chapter 4, verse 17, NIV).

Saul's feigned humility at his first meeting with Samuel soon gave way to self-awareness, bordering on arrogance, as soon as he became king.

Most times negligence arises out of undue familiarity with the things of God, or on experiences.

Perhaps he had counsellors urging him to behave like the king he was! Who was Samuel to be dictating to him, when he was a mere subject of His Majesty the King! He quickly forgot his beginnings; hence, Samuel would frequently preface his messages to Saul with a reminder that he was the one whom God had sent to crown him king.

Pride does lead to a fall (Proverbs Chapter 11, verse 2) and the first casualty of pride is our reverence for our leaders, parents or benefactors.

Like the Church in Ephesus, we are admonished not to forsake our first love (Revelation Chapter 2, verse 4).

Today's Church must never lose sight of the Source of its strength – obedience to the word of God, and adherence to the guidance of the Holy Spirit.

As Christians, we must ensure that we pay attention to the details of God's instructions and obey them. We must never presume upon God's grace and love because God never speaks in vain, and the full implication of His instructions may dawn on us when it is already too late!

6

ஃ JONAH ఇ;

HEADSTRONG AND SELFISH

The story of Jonah reads like a movie script, but God did not put it in the Bible just for the purpose of entertainment.

Jonah was simply introduced as the son of Amittai, accompanied by God's instruction for him to *'Go to the great city of Nineveh and preach against it, because its wickedness has come up before Me.'* (Jonah Chapter 1, verses 1 to 2).

However, in 2Kings Chapter 14, verses 24 and 25 NLT, King Jeroboam II (793 – 753 BC) was reported to have *recovered the territories of Israel between Lebo-hamath and the Dead Sea, just as the LORD the God of*

Israel had promised through Jonah, the son of Amittai, the prophet from Gath-hepher."

Jonah was from the Northern Region of Israel, near Nazareth, which later become the hometown of the LORD Jesus Christ. Jonah was therefore a pre-exilic prophet of note.

The ensuing drama is racy and hilarious even though it was of serious spiritual significance.

Upon hearing God's instruction, Jonah set out on a journey in the opposite direction; instead of heading to Nineveh, he embarked on a ship to Tarshish. Instead of travelling North-east for about 1,200 kilometres to Niniveh in Modern-day Syria, he travelled in the opposite direction, heading for Tashish which was almost 5,000 kilometres away in Modern-day Spain.

'Go to the great city of Nineveh and preach against it'

Evidently, Jonah wanted to go as far away as possible from God's instruction and purpose for his life! He boarded a ship at Joppa, heading west. Soon after the ship set sail, God sent a mighty storm that buffeted the ship violently.

The desperate sailors called on their insensate gods, and threw cargo into the sea to lighten its load so it would not sink, yet the storm grew worse! Meanwhile, Jonah was sound asleep in the hold of the ship!

The Captain was exasperated to find someone sleeping in the middle of such a calamitous crisis. He woke him up and shouted at him to call on his own God for mercy.

The crewmembers cast lots to find out who was bringing misfortune and endangering the lives of the crew and passengers, and the ship itself.

The lot fell on Jonah. I firmly believe God was at work here and influenced whichever method those pagans chose, in order to push Jonah to his destiny.

Jonah soon confessed that he was running away from the assignment given to him by *'the LORD, the God of heaven, Who made the sea and the land'* (Jonah Chapter 1, verse 9).

Upon hearing God's instruction, Jonah set out on a journey in the opposite direction; instead of heading to Nineveh

This greatly terrified the sailors, and when the storm grew even worse, they asked what they should do. Jonah made a radical decision that they should throw him overboard so that the storm could stop.

However, the sailors refused to carry out such a terrible act, and put in all their skills to steady their ship but the stormy sea became more violent. The sailors then cried out to the LORD, the God of Jonah, asking for forgiveness for their decision to throw Jonah overboard. Then they picked Jonah up and threw him into the raging sea, and the storm stopped at once!

Jonah must have imagined himself drowning and sinking to the bottom of the sea, but he soon found himself in the first submarine transport vehicle ever made!

God had arranged for a whale (or a giant fish or sea creature) to swallow Jonah. Jonah was conscious while he was in the belly of the fish for three days, and realised his predicament.

The lot fell on Jonah. I firmly believe God was at work here

He cried out to God for help, pleading for His mercy. God relented, and on the third day, God ordered the fish to spit up Jonah on the beach, and it did (Jonah Chapter 2, verse 10).

The LORD then repeated His instruction to Jonah:

"Get up and go to the great city of Nineveh, and deliver the message of judgment I have given you" (Jonah Chapter 3, verse 1).

This time, Jonah obeyed the LORD's command and went to Nineveh. Jonah shouted to the crowds: 'Forty days from now Nineveh will be destroyed!' The people of Nineveh, from the king to the ordinary man immediately put on sackcloth, fasted and repented of their evil ways. God then had mercy and withheld disaster from them.

According to Encyclopaedia Britannica, Nineveh was the oldest and most popular city of the ancient Assyrian empire, situated on the east bank of the Tigris River and encircled by the modern city of Mosul, Iraq. Wikipedia also says that Nineveh was the largest city in the world for several decades, with a population of about 120,000. The Bible records that it was 'an exceedingly great city of three days' journey in breadth.'

One would have thought that as a man who had the Spirit of God in him, that Jonah would be delighted at the great success of his crusade in Nineveh.

Instead, immediately he realised that God had relented from punishing Nineveh, Jonah became very angry (Jonah Chapter 4, verse 1).

He complained about God's compassion and steadfast love, and said that he had earlier decided to go to Tarshish because he knew that God would have compassion on Nineveh.

He haughtily went to the city side, to await what God would do to the city. He made a shelter, and God arranged for a leafy plant to grow there and provide shade for Jonah, who felt very comfortable.

However, God, however, allowed a worm to destroy the plant, such that by the next day, it had withered away. The LORD then turned up the heat of the sun to scorch Jonah who became despondent that the plant that had given him shade had died. When God questioned whether he was angry because of the plant that died, Jonah retorted, *'Yes, even angry enough to die!'* (Jonah Chapter 4, verse 9).

Then the LORD said to him:

"You feel sorry about the plant, though you did nothing to put it there. It came quickly and died quickly. But Nineveh has more than 120,000 people living in spiritual darkness, not to mention all the animals. Should not I feel sorry for such a great city?" (Jonah Chapter 4, verses 10 to 11 NIV)

This rebuke from the LORD sums up Jonah's attitude to the Kingdom project. He did not want the people of Nineveh to receive God's mercy because he felt they did not deserve it.

One would have thought that as a man who had the Spirit of God in him, that Jonah would be delighted at the great success of his crusade in Nineveh

Instead of being happy that the sinful city had repented, he was angry because he believed they deserved nothing but divine retribution for all their evil deeds against Israel.

Nineveh was the chief city of the Assyrian Empire that was a perpetual enemy of Israel, and which eventually sacked the Northern Kingdom and swept everyone into exile in 722BC.

Many modern Christians are not different from Jonah. Like the Laodicean Church, we are self-righteous, believing that we are spiritually superior to those we perceive as hopeless sinners.

We wish that such people who have done so much wrong to us should never come to the saving knowledge of Christ.

Of course, we have every human reason to wish retribution for those who have maltreated us or who have persecuted the Church of Christ, as has happened indifferent parts of the world.

Imagine what would be the reaction of many Christians or Churches if God instructed them to preach to Islamic terrorists like Al Qaeda, Al Shabbab or Boko Haram leaders. Knowing the overwhelming grace of God, we would likely be reluctant to preach for the repentance of such people

Instead of being happy that the sinful city had repented, (Jonah) was angry because he believed they deserved nothing but divine retribution for all their evil deeds against Israel

who are guilty of the gruesome death and torture of many Christians around the world.

God is not man! His ways are not our ways, and His thoughts not our thoughts (Isaiah Chapter 55, verse 9). God's mercies are like the never-ending sea, full and available to all.

It is the will of God that all men should come to the saving knowledge of Christ.

We therefore have a duty to align with God's purpose and do the work of evangelism no matter where it takes us. We owe our salvation to the fact that God's mercy was available to us in the days of our sinning.

Our hearts can become so calloused by our prejudices that we lose sight of God's commandment for us to go and make disciples of all nations. It is so easy to be overwhelmed by the wickedness of people around us that we lose our empathy about the plight and the needs of all men – no matter how evil they might be – for salvation.

Many modern Christians are not different from Jonah…we are self-righteous, believing that we are spiritually superior to those we perceive as hopeless sinners

Let us not, like Jonah, hold material things more important than human lives. God values every human soul, and so should we.

7

℘ ANANIAS AND SAPPHIRA ℘:

SELF DECEPTION - ACTS 5:1-11

The story of Ananias actually starts from Chapter 4 of the Acts of the Apostles, verses 32 to 36. The first believers were united in hand and mind, and shared everything they had freely with one another.

The wealthy ones among them sold their landed properties and houses, and brought the proceeds to the Apostles to give to those in need.

One outstanding example of this generosity was Joseph, a Levite, whom the Apostles nicknamed 'Barnabas', Son of Encouragement. He had sold a field he owned and brought the money to the Apostles.

This selfless and sacrificial giving by Barnabas must have stirred the hearts of the first Church, such that many began to give out of their resources for the good of all. They indeed desired a community in which there was unity, oneness of mind and altruistic care for everyone.

Ananias and Sapphira were obviously well-known as members of this first congregation of Christians, and they must have felt challenged by the selfless example of Barnabas. They also craved the accolades of the Apostles, the way Barnabas was nicknamed, 'Son of Encouragement' because of his exemplary generosity of spirit.

The first believers were united in hand and mind, and shared everything they had freely with one another.

Ananias and Sapphira wanted to emulate Barnabas; they agreed to sell their property and to bring the full proceeds to the Apostles' feet.

However, after the sales, perhaps looking at the size of the proceeds, they began to develop cold feet, and the idea of cutting corners loomed large in their minds, and soon took a life of its own. They decided to keep a part of the proceeds but to lie to the Apostles that they had brought everything.

Ananias, the man of the house, proudly strutted to Apostle Peter, and must have announced in a loud voice how himself and his wife had been generous enough to sell their property and to bring all the proceeds for the care of the less privileged ones, just like Barnabas and some others had done. Ananias must have beamed expectantly when Apostle Peter stood up to speak. Instead of commendation, he was stung by the sharp rebuke of Peter.

Ananias, the man of the house, proudly strutted to Apostle Peter

"Ananias, why has Satan filled your heart to lie to the Holy Spirit and keep back part of the price of the land yourself? While it remained, was it not your own? And after it was sold, was it not in your own control? Why have you conceived this thing in your heart? You have not lied to men, but to God." (Acts Chapter 5, verse 3 to 4 NKJV).

Ananias' heart froze within his chest and turned to stone; and he fell dead at the feet of Apostle Peter. This caused great fear among the audience.

Peter's stinging words convey an object lesson for Christians of all ages:

(1)   God does not force any of us to make a vow, neither does He judge us by the actions of other Christians;

(2)   God does not covet our material possessions; indeed, He is the Owner of all things (Psalm

Chapter 50, verse 9 to 13; Haggai Chapter 2, verse 8);

(3)   Our possessions are ours to dispose as we like, but once we decide to give some to the LORD we must ensure that we keep our vow;

(4)   It is the greatest travesty to try to deceive God by presenting less than we vowed while claiming that we have given all;

(5)   We may not fall and die as Ananias did, but the spiritual consequences are equally dire.

I have often wondered where Sapphira was for three hours that she did not hear of the fate that had befallen her co-conspirator husband. Perhaps she was taking her time to dress up for the big occasion, and choosing the best time to make a grand entrance to get the expected applause. Perhaps she was using some of the money they had kept back to sort out some urgent family matter. We may never know until eternity reveals everything.

Anyway, three hours after her husband's burial, Sapphira arrived. Peter gave her the opportunity to redeem her life, but she repeated the deception she had agreed with her husband. Her judgment was instant too and she died on the spot.

There is nothing hidden from the sight of the LORD. He sees our thoughts even before they enter our hearts, and fully comprehends our ways (Psalm Chapter 139, verse 2 to 4).

There is so much self-deception and hypocrisy in the Church today. Many Christians are so preoccupied with petty jealousies, envy and competition. The Church has become a market place for bazaars, flamboyant display of wealth and unhealthy rivalries.

People outdo each other in making pledges and announcing donations in order to impress fellow Christians or Pastors. Many of such pledges or vows are never redeemed, nor were they intended to be redeemed.

The first Church tackled this problem head-on with the Power of the Holy Spirit, and the Authority of the LORD Jesus Christ.

The Church has become a market place for bazaars, flamboyant display of wealth and unhealthy rivalries.

Unfortunately, many of today's Churches are mere human organisations, neither yielded to, nor controlled by the Holy Spirit. Instead of Godliness and contentment, the ethos of much of the modern day Church is worldliness and covetousness.

Our gifts are for the edification of the Church and for the Glory of God. We should give as a matter of course, with simplicity and discretion. We should not be stampeded by the actions of acts of generosity of others.

The highest giver may be the pastor's favourite, but such a person may be very far from God. The LORD gave us a profound example with the story of the widow's mites in Mark Chapter 12, verse 41 to 44.

The LORD is coming back for the faithful Church, not a 'wealthy' or prosperous Church.

There is already a scarcity of the word of God on many pulpits; rather there is a surfeit of social gospel, motivational speeches, a huge dose of New Age mysticism and syncretism, masquerading as Church.

> The highest giver may be the pastor's favourite, but such a person may be very far from God.

Modern day Church leaders need to follow the example of the Apostle Peter and firmly set the feet of their members on the Way of the Cross.

The spirit of Ananias and Sapphira should not be allowed to gain grounds in the Church. Indeed the house of God should be a place of worship, not a place for buying and selling.

Fund raising for church work or missions should not be a raucous affair. The example laid down by the Apostle Paul in 1Corinthians Chapter 16, verse 2 should suffice:

"On the first day of the week let each one of you lay something aside, storing up as he may prosper, that there be no collections when I come." NKJV

The times in which we live demand a church that is heaven-centred, and conduct that honours our LORD and Saviour, Jesus Christ.

An atmosphere that creates room for competition in material things, covetousness and petty jealousies is undesirable.

8

৸THE SEVEN SONS OF SCEVA৹

TAKING THE NAME OF THE LORD IN VAIN
ACTS CHAPTER 19, VERSE 11 TO 20

The seven sons of Sceva were part of itinerant Jews who went about exorcising disease-causing demons in the region of Ephesus.

At that material time, Apostle Paul was ministering in Ephesus, and the Power of God was being mightily demonstrated in mass conversions, healings and the breaking of the power of demons.

"Now God worked unusual miracles by the hands of Paul, so that even handkerchiefs or aprons were brought from his body to the sick, and the diseases left them and the evil spirits went out of them."

(Acts Chapter 19, verse 11 to 12).

According to Rabbi Geoffrey Dennis, "Exorcism is a ritual of power performed in order to drive an evil spirit, whether demonic or ghostly, from a possessed person, location, or object."

First Century Romano-Jewish Chronicler Flavius Josephus recounts incidents of possession and exorcism in his **Antiques of the Jews**. In his description, exorcism involved burning herbs and immersing the possessed person in water. The Dead Sea Scrolls include several exorcism incantations and formulae, mostly directed against disease-causing demons.

You can then imagine the amazement of these professional exorcists when they saw Paul casting out demons only in the Name of Jesus! They simply adapted it as additional formula, and started calling the Name of the LORD Jesus over those hard evil spirits, *saying,* **"We exorcise you by the Jesus Whom Paul preaches."** (Acts Chapter 19, verse 13b).

The seven sons of Sceva, a Jewish chief priest, also adopted the new formula. They soon encountered a stubborn demon who confronted them when they tried using 'the Name of Jesus Whom Paul preaches.'

"And the evil spirit answered them and said, 'Jesus I know, and Paul I know; but who are you?'" (Acts Chapter 19, verse 15 NKJV).

What followed was a disgraceful and thorough beating of the seven brothers by the demon-possessed man. They fled the house naked and wounded. This invariably led to a region-wide revival with many believing and receiving Jesus as LORD and Saviour.

"Also, many of those who had practised magic brought their books together and burned them in the sight of all…" (Acts Chapter 19, verse 19).

The Jewish exorcists fully recognised the futility of their incantations and submitted to the Lordship of Jesus.

The story of the sons of Sceva presents a picture of many modern day Christians and Churches. Every Christian acknowledges that there is Power in the Name of Jesus, and that with the help of the Holy Spirit we can accomplish so much.

However, for many, the Name of Jesus is more of a formula, which they can chant to ward off evil or receive Divine assistance. They instinctively shout 'Jesus' at any sign of danger but in reality, they are not committed to Him and their hearts are far from Him.

The Apostle Paul describes such people as *'having a form of godliness but denying its power …'* (2Timothy Chapter 3, verse 5).

The Apostle Jude was more scathing in his description of such people:

"These are spots in your love feasts, while they feast with you without fear, serving only themselves. They are clouds without water, carried about by the winds; late autumn trees without fruit, twice dead, pulled up by the roots; raging waves of the sea, foaming up their own shame; wandering stars for whom is reserved the blackness of darkness forever." (Jude Chapter 12, verse 13).

In the Old Testament, Prophet Elisha performed the most miracles – 16 – double the number for Elijah. Gehazi was Elisha's right hand man who spent much time with the Man of God. Yet, he was in the water but very dry!

In II Kings Chapter 4, verses 18 to 37, we read about the death and restoration of the son of the Shunammite woman who was a beneficiary of one of Elisha's miracles.

The son that had come by prophecy suddenly took ill and died. The woman did not grieve openly, but carefully laid the body of her son on the bed she had

ℐℑ

They instinctively shout 'Jesus' at any sign of danger but in reality, they are not committed to Him and their hearts are far from Him.

provided for Elisha. Then she saddled a donkey and went to meet the prophet.

After listening to her bitter cry about the loss of her son, Elisha had instructed his servant, Gehazi, to take his staff and go touch the child so he would be resuscitated. However, the woman insisted that the Man of God must go with her. Obviously, she had little faith in Gehazi's spiritual qualifications.

In any case, while they were still on the way, Gehazi ran ahead and laid the staff of Elisha on the child, hoping to receive Elisha and the woman with a 'Voila!'

Gehazi was Elisha's right hand man who spent much time with the Man of God. Yet, he was in the water but very dry!

"Now Gehazi went on ahead of them, and laid the staff on the face of the child; but there was neither voice nor hearing. Therefore he went back to meet him, and told him, saying, "'The child has not awakened.'"
II Kings Chapter 4, verse 31 NKJV).

The seven sons of Sceva were just as empty as Gehazi. He walked with Elisha but he had a different agenda. He never imbibed the values of the Prophet, nor was he desirous of partaking of the anointing on Elisha.

He did not have the same thirst for the Holy Spirit as Elisha, who had requested for a double portion of

Elijah's anointing, when asked to request for what was dearest to him. (I Kings Chapter 2, verse 9).

The effect of the spirit of Gehazi and the sons of Sceva is the spirit of materialism and covetousness as we see in II Kings Chapter 5. Anyone trying to imitate Christian virtues without the indwelling of the Holy Spirit runs an uphill task — so much exertion and pain, with little result.

Invoking the Name of Jesus without a saving knowledge and surrender to Jesus is a dangerous way of life. There are many sons of Sceva parading as preachers of the Gospel of Christ today. They voraciously call out the Name of Jesus without the contrition and submission to the Holy Spirit that is required to be a disciple of Jesus. They blend the Name of Jesus into their purely materialistic motivational speeches and present them as sermons.

> The seven sons of Sceva were just as empty as Gehazi.
>
> He did not have the same thirst for the Holy Spirit as Elisha

The Apostle Paul preaches against empty religiosity in Romans Chapter 12, verses 1 and 2, and affirms that the only way to spiritual transformation and is by total yieldedness to the Holy Spirit.

The Church is at ease because of the mercy of God, which allows the weeds to grow with the wheat.

(Mathew Chapter 13, verse 24 to 30).

The airwaves and church pulpits are inundated daily with voices of many men ostensibly proclaiming the words of God.

Many make 'prophetic' statements which are, at best, clever guesses based on current events, or so generalist in nature that they can claim fulfilment of their 'prophesies' based on the tiniest shred of credence.

For example, in 2020, the year the Coronavirus shut down the whole world, no prophet foresaw it. However, some began to claim that they had made allusions to it in their prophesies in general terms.

For 2020, most Nigerian 'prophets' predicted a year of plenty, prosperity and buoyancy. One of them said that in 2020, 'earthquakes and volcanoes that have been dormant for years will erupt.'

The United States Geological Survey (USGS) for 2020 debunked all that. The year actually had the least number of earthquakes in years, and very few were up to magnitude 6.5 on the Richter Scale.

The typical Nigerian prophecy is often about serious

illness or demise of prominent people like former presidents or traditional rulers who are already advanced in age!

The social media are replete with stories of untoward methods used by many so-called men of God in their quest for power, growth, prosperity and influence. Many claim to perform miracles for people who turn out to be paid fakes, or who later die of the diseases they claimed they had cured.

Indeed many Sons of Sceva parade themselves as pastors all over the place shouting the Name of Jesus, with whom they have no personal relationship.

Nowadays, we hear of 'hyper-grace; superior grace; higher grace' and all such, which are designed to cover up sinful habits - adultery, stealing, domestic violence, divorce, authoritarianism that do not jell with Biblical injunctions. Unfortunately, many people are daily misled by these men:

"Whose end is destruction, whose god is their belly, and whose glory is in their shame – who set their mind on earthly things." (Philippians Chapter 3, verse 19 NKJV)

However, the time of harvest will come when the wheat will be separated from the tares. Matthew Chapter 13, verse 24 to 30

The hypocrites in Zion have every reason to be afraid:

"The sinners in Zion are afraid;
Fearfulness has seized the hypocrite:
'Who among us shall dwell with the devouring fire?
Who among us shall dwell with everlasting burnings?'

He who walks righteously and speaks uprightly,
He who despises the gain of oppressions,
Who gestures with his hand, refusing bribes,
Who stops his ears from hearing of bloodshed,
And shuts his eyes from seeing evil:

He will dwell on high;
His place of defence will be the fortress of rocks;
Bread will be given him,
His water will be sure" **(Isaiah Chapter 33, verse 14 to 16 NKJV);**

The Laodicean Church was much like the sons of Sceva – they liked the esteem and power that came from being in Christ, but lacked the discipline and commitment to be a true Church of Christ, neither hot nor cold.

They had an illusion of greatness whereas they were pathetically wretched. That is also the true picture of much of today's Church, sadly.

He, who has an ear, let him hear what the Spirit is saying to the churches.

9

❧ THE GENERATIONS ☙

PROVERBS CHAPTER 30, VERSES 11 TO 14

"There is a generation that curses its father, and does not bless its mother. There is a generation that is pure in its own eyes, yet is not washed from its filthiness. There is a generation – oh, how lofty are their eyes! And their eyelids are lifted up. There is a generation whose teeth are like swords, and whose fangs are like knives, to devour the poor from off the earth, and the needy from among men."

Proverbs 30 is tilted 'The Wisdom of Agur', further described as the son of Jakeh. He apparently dictated or recited the proverbs to Ithiel and Ucal. The words of Agur are filled with observations on life and the natural world, inviting us to look again at the world around us with the eyes of faith.

He started with self-deprecation: ***"Surely I am more stupid than any man, and do not have the understanding of a man. I neither learned wisdom nor have knowledge of the Holy One."*** Proverbs Chapter 30, verse 2 to 3.

According to Spurgeon, Agur was making it clear that he was not relying on human philosophy or learning, but fully on faith in God and the revelation of the Holy Spirit. In other words, he was just a vessel of God, ascribing all the glory to God, and not himself.

In Verse 4, he emphasises God's pre-eminence and that of His Son - Jesus Christ when he asked a series of rhetorical questions.

Then in Verses 5 to 6, Agur emphasises the purity, strength and integrity of the word of God, prays for personal integrity in Verses 7 to 9, and admonishes against speaking ill of other people in Verse 10.

Our interest is in Verses 11 to 14, where Agur describes the 'generations.'

According to the Oxford Advanced English Dictionary, 'Generation' means:

- All the people living at the same time or approximately the same age
- It could also mean peer group, people of similar inclinations or cultural values.

Most Bible commentaries agree that the 'generations' in this passage refers to four kinds of people that are discernible in every age of human existence, and everywhere.

1. ***There is a generation that curses its father and does not bless its mother***: this represents the generation of young people who have no respect for their parents. They are self-conceited, proud, headstrong, irreverent and despiteful of their parents. We see such people all around us, even in our churches!

   How many parents have lamented that their children no longer listen to them or obey their instructions! In the age in which we live, such children generally consign their parents to 'old school', meaning, ignorant, out of touch, technologically illiterate, or bound by moral strictures that no longer apply in an age of relativity.

For such a generation, there is no absolute right or wrong, no absolute morality or immorality, it all depends on how you choose to interpret the situation. Unfortunately, many churches have been torn apart because their young ones fail to see eye-to-eye with their parents or the older generation concerning Biblical standards for personal conduct. Young people openly challenge their elders and even their Pastors!

There is a new attitude of defiance and irreverence

among a certain generation of young people, products of a second generation of lukewarm Christians who never had time to teach their children the precepts of God, or did so lackadaisically.

Many have not modelled Christian virtues to their children; their pontifications have very little effect on their children once they become teenagers or when they leave home for school and therefore become more independent.

Many Christian parents are so devoted to career successes and pursuits that they have ceded their parental responsibilities to the schools, housemaids and children teachers in church. Some are even so busy in church that they hardly have time for their primary ministry - their families.

For such a generation, there is no absolute right or wrong, no absolute morality or immorality,

The age of materialism and relativity have compounded the problems for many Christian parents not deeply grounded in the Christian doctrine. They themselves are carried about by every wind of doctrine, and thus bequeath undone cake to their children.

When such children are further contaminated by the world system, they become prey to all kinds of ideas which are mixed up with Christian beliefs and practices, thereby creating the kind of hard heartedness we see among certain of the younger generation who believe they owe no gratitude to their parents and no duty of care.

Some have become rebels and in open opposition to their parents.

Unfortunately, most of the modern churches have become organisations, rather than spiritual organisms. Emphasis is on routine programmes and grandiose projects without any effort to measure or even care about their spiritual quotient. Church members become prominent by turning up at various programmes, and not because of their spiritual growth.

Pastors have continued to lose their authority because their counsels have proven, over time, to be mere human wisdom, rather than wisdom from above. The younger generations see the pretensions of their parents and spiritual leaders, and become disinterested and disrespectful.

This is the sad state of much of today's Christian church and Christian families.

Many Christian parents are so devoted to career successes and pursuits that they have ceded their parental responsibilities

"Train up a child in the way he should go, and when he is old he will not depart from it." Proverbs Chapter 22, verse 6 NKJV

To train a child implies teaching them the precepts of God (Deuteronomy Chapter 6, verse 7). *You shall teach them diligently to your children, and shall talk of them when you sit in your house, when you walk by the way, when you lie down and when you rise up.*

You train your children by **teaching** them diligently. Your relationship with your children at home should also **mirror** the words of God. You should **model** Christ in your daily walk with your children, in your values, your conduct in the midst of other people, your ambitions, and your principles. You should also ensure that you teach your children through your daily submission to God at bedtime and when you rise to face the day.

This simple injunction in Proverbs Chapter 22, verse 6 is not as simple as it sounds. It is quite complicated, and failure to pass this test is at the heart of the rebellious generation that has sprung up in our midst.

2. *There is a generation that is pure in its own eyes, yet is not washed from its filthiness.*

    This refers to the stratum of our society that is self-righteous. They are uppity about their piety and closeness to God, yet they are truly empty vessels. Such people are marked out by their spiritual arrogance, which they have acquired through their age in church, their positions in society, their wealth and influence.

They are the ones that dictate church policies and directions, and insist on the letters of church constitutions and byelaws and letting it be known that they are for rectitude and the rule of law!

Such people are the terrors of Pastors and other spiritual leaders, who must kow-tow to them, or find the church ungovernable.

They are the church elders, even deacons and trustees, who have lost the capacity for learning daily from the Holy Spirit, but rather believe they know enough to lead others. They are the ones that relish in church organisation and politics.

They are uppity about their piety and closeness to God, yet they are truly empty vessels.

The Apostle Jude refers to such people thus:

"These are spots in your love feasts, while they feast with you without fear, serving only themselves. They are clouds without water, carried about by the winds; late autumn trees without fruit, twice dead, pulled up by the roots..." **Jude Chapter 12.**

Such people, while proclaiming faith in Christ are, in reality, apostates who have left their first love and adopted strange doctrines.

Every church has such people; and pastors have a duty of care to them. Pastors have to design special teachings for certain kinds of members who run the risk of becoming spiritually complacent, and covering up their emptiness through church activities, donations, constant availability and other humanly laudable actions.

Every member of the church must continually learn submission, diligence, obedience, spiritual fruitfulness, righteous living, fear of God, not just through formal training and programmes, but also through deliberate spiritual exercises aimed at ensuring fresh anointing.

Pastors must constantly preach repentance from sin, the daily repentance of the believers, the significance of the Cross and the Ministry of the Holy Spirit.

Each Christian should also daily exercise himself or herself to ensure that we do not take the word of God for granted. We must daily yield our bodies as a living sacrifice, holy and acceptable to God; we must ensure that we are constantly firmly grafted in the True Vine Who gives us nourishment; we must be diligent students of the word of God, and apply them in our daily lives.

The Church in Laodicea had some dangerous assumptions:

'They were rich and wealthy, and had need of nothing.'

However, the LORD said that on the contrary, they were:

- Wretched
- Miserable
- Poor
- Blind, and
- Naked

How do you see your Church today? How do you think the LORD sees your Church? Who dominates and rules over your church? How does your Church measure good membership?

3. ***There is a generation whose teeth are like swords, and whose fangs are like knives, to devour the poor off the earth, and the needy from among men.***

We can all easily identify this group of people, who are ruthless about their pursuit of wealth and personal gain. Such people believe that whatever they have achieved in life was by their own hard work or accident of birth, and have no patience or sympathy with those who are less endowed.

Even in church, such people have no sympathy for the poor, they would rather recommend that people work harder, which is not bad counsel, but it is given with the impression that all they did to be successful was hard work. Perhaps such people should ask the truck pusher, the head loader, that woman that straps her baby on her back and trudges all over town, selling a few condiments to make a living for her family! We must never lose sight of the abundant grace of God upon our lives as Christians.

We must never forget the immortal words of the 16th Century Christian Martyr, John Bradford, who on seeing a poor criminal led to execution, exclaimed: 'But for the Grace of God, there goes John Bradford!'

Many years back, a sister in the church I was attending then, made such disparaging remarks about another sister who had come to ask her for some money to feed her family. Her reply: 'you people should know that people like us work hard for the money. I do not pick money by the road side.

Even in church, such people have no sympathy for the poor

You should also find something to do instead of coming to church to constitute a nuisance.' You could have cut the collective breath held by those of us around them with a knife! Mercifully, other brethren rallied round the 'poor' sister, and some actually told off the uppity one, who went on to become a Pastor in the same church!

However, this group more properly describes those who go about preying on the weaknesses of the poor among us, widows, children and the disabled, to cheat them of their rightful possessions, and to enrich themselves with ill-gotten wealth.

In some cultures, once a man dies, the family or community immediately accuses the widow of being responsible for his death, no matter how illogical it might sound. They do this in order to justify the cruelty and evil they will later mete on the poor widow and her children, especially if the children are still young.

The immediate relatives of the deceased would seize all the documents to the man's property they could find, demand his bank account details from his widow, and even throw the poor woman out of the house she may have built with her husband. In some cases, all these take place while the dead man has not even been buried. The saddest part is that many Christians are involved in these obnoxious practices!

We live in a world that has increasingly become more cynical, untrusting, untruthful and treacherous. It has become more dangerous to be kind and good to others. However, we as Christians should not allow the system and values of the world to harden us and make us uncaring and unmindful of the suffering of people around us.

We must do as much good as the Holy Spirit leads us to do. Disappointments, ingratitude, betrayals, backstabbing and other forms of hostility should not deter us from doing good, because we serve a God Who sees and is able to protect and compensate us when we suffer loss because we are obeying and imitating Him in love.

These 'generations' are part of our daily reality, and we find their tribe in every facet of life, including in the household of faith. One of the biggest problems confronting today's church is materialism. Pastors have managed to make materialism spiritual by emphasising the importance of 'giving', and by mindless acquisition of money and other comforts of life. Materialism and spirituality cannot mix because they are like oil and water! The LORD Jesus Christ warned against it when He admonished:

"No one can serve two masters; for either he will hate the one and love the other, or else he will be loyal to the one and despise the other. You cannot serve God and mammon." Matthew Chapter 6, verse 42, Luke Chapter 16, verse 13.

This basic characteristic disqualified the two sons of Samuel from being accepted as judges in Israel. Joel and Abiah were accused of not walking in his (Samuel's) ways, ***'but turned after lucre, and took bribes, and perverted judgment.'*** 1Samuel Chapter 8, verse 3. That was the major reason the elders of Israel demanded that Samuel should give them a king.

The Apostles warned against the negative impact of materialism on the church, especially among Pastors. Paul admonished that Bishops or Pastors should not be given to 'filthy lucre' among other qualities; same for deacons (1Timothy Chapter 3 verses 3 and 8; Titus Chapter 1, verse 7)

Apostle Peter also warned in 1Peter Chapter 5, verse 2 to 3:

"Feed the flock of God which is among you, taking the oversight thereof, not by constraint, but willingly; not for filthy lucre, but of a ready mind; Neither as being lords over God's heritage, but being examples to the flock." KJV

According to AW Tozer, in a Sermon Titled: 'Desire and the End of the Age',

"Another reason for the absence of real yearning for Christ's return is that Christians are so comfortable in this world that they have little desire to leave it. For those leaders who set the pace of religion and determine its content and quality, Christianity has become of late remarkably lucrative. The streets of gold do not have too great an appeal for those who find it so easy to pile up gold and silver in the service of the LORD here on earth."

This is a dire warning to all Christians, especially to those who are Pastors and Leaders of the church.

In the midst of so much crass materialism, the faithful Christian must keep in mind what kind of generation he ought and should belong to:

"But you are a CHOSEN GENERATION, a ROYAL

PRIESTHOOD, a HOLY NATION, (GOD'S) OWN SPECIAL PEOPLE that you may proclaim the praises of Him Who called you out of darkness into His marvellous light."
(1Peter Chapter 2, verse 9 NKJV)

What are the implications of this?

i. We have been called out of the various generations of this world to become God's chosen Generation - a tribe of people whose values are very different from the values of the other co-existing generations. We are to be identified and distinguished by our 'differentness', and we must take care that by our conduct, choices and values, we are not mistaken as part of the generations of this world.

In the midst of so much crass materialism, the faithful Christian must keep in mind what kind of generation he ought and should belong to

Three qualities distinguish anyone who is part of God's chosen Generation:
holiness,
gratitude and
yieldedness to the Holy Spirit.

-Holiness entails striving to be like Christ in character, disposition, speech and values; not by mere profession but as a way of life authenticated by inner assurance and the testimony of others.

-A life of gratitude to God is a life that is lived delicately and with great discretion, to avoid offending our Master Who paid the price for the freedom we enjoy. It is a life of 'thanks-living', devoted to extolling God's goodness in our speech, our choices and our relationships.

-To live a life of yieldedness to the Holy Spirit is to live with eternity in view (Ecclesiastes Chapter 3, verse 11). It is to daily make our bodies a living sacrifice to God, impervious to the allures of the world (Romans Chapter 12, verses 1 to 2), and conscious of pleasing Him in all things.

ii. We are a ROYAL PRIESTHOOD, expected to continually minister praise, worship and adoration before the LORD. Priests are also expected to be dedicated to the service of God, to stand in the gap for the church, the nation and our world; to offer prayers on behalf of self and others, and to be the voice of God on earth.

As priests, we have direct access and fellowship with God, and are also called to expand the Kingdom of God and influence the world like a king. Our royalty and our priesthood derive directly from our LORD Jesus Christ Who is our King and the Great High Priest.

iii.   We are GOD'S SPECIAL PEOPLE, because God takes special interest in us because of our lifestyle. The world does not take kindly to anyone that want to be different from it.

A Kingdom lifestyle will necessarily attract resentment, hatred, envy, sabotage and persecution. Nevertheless, the LORD counsels us to be of good cheer because He has overcome the world. (John Chapter 16, verse 33).

These qulities will certainly make Christians out as different; our lives will display the goodness of God, proclaiming the praises and glory of God in our daily living.

> A Kingdom lifestyle will necessarily attract resentment, hatred, envy, sabotage and persecution

People will see God's goodness in our lives, and note that we are not living like them, in dread of the systems and values of the world. They will come to us for solutions, and we then point them to the Cross and the matchless Grace of God that sustains us in the midst of a perverse world.

"Most assuredly, I say to you, he who believes in Me, the works that I do, he will do also; and greater

works than these he will do, because I go to My Father. And whatever you ask in My Name, that I will do, that the Father may be glorified in the Son." John Chapter 14, verse 13 NKJV

What a blessed generation is God's chosen generation!

More marvellous and more glorious than all the generations of this world!

A generation that enjoys righteous, peace and joy in the Holy Spirit!

A generation that disdains this world - with its allures of evil and wickedness!

The kingdoms of this world will surely become the Kingdom of God, our Father and of His Christ!

Maranatha!

10

ೞ LOOK AT THE FIG TREE ೞ:

PROVERBS CHAPTER 30, VERSES 11 TO 14

The fig tree was a fruit tree native to the Mediterranean Region. It had the characteristic of yielding fruits two seasons in the same year. It provided nourishment to both rich and poor, and was evidence of the abundant provisions of God for His people.

The LORD Jesus Christ often used the fig tree in teaching about the dangers of hypocrisy and foolhardy Christianity in so many parables. Indeed the fig tree appears in so many teachings about the relationship between the believer and our Creator.

At the cusp of the fall of man and the demonstration of God's undying compassion, in **Genesis Chapter 3, verse 7**, God used the leaves of the fig tree to cover the nakedness and shame of Adam and Eve, and the fig tree features throughout the Bible.

The fig tree is symptomatic of the expectations of God from His children, and illustrates the LORD's admonition that we should be the salt of the earth and light of the world.

The leaves of the fig tree were used for covering nakedness (Genesis Chapter 3, verse 7); and providing shade (John Chapter 1:48 and 50).

The fruit was used for food (1Samuel Chapter 30:12); sent as present (1Samuel Chapter 25:18); and used for healing (Isaiah Chapter 38, verse 21)

The LORD expects fruit from His church, not mere posturing

Other references to the fig tree include Deuteronomy Chapter 8, verse 8, Judges Chapter 9, verse 10 to 11, Proverbs Chapter 27, verse 18, Jeremiah Chapter 8, verse 13 and Joel Chapter 1, 7 to 12, to mention a few.No wonder that God takes exception when the fig tree fails to yield its fruit.

The Parables of the Barren Fig Tree (Luke 13:6-9)

In this Parable, the LORD tells the story of a man who had planted a fig tree in his vineyard. Over a period of three years, he came seeking fruit from the tree, but it had yielded none.

In frustration, he ordered the vine keeper to cut down the tree, but the keeper pleaded with the master to allow him dig around and fertilize the tree one more season, after which he would cut it down if it still failed to bear fruit.

The church of God is like that fig tree. The LORD expects fruit from His church, not mere posturing. Time is running out; the day of reckoning is very close.

The Wheat and the Tares (Matthew Chapter 13, verses 23 to 43)

The LORD Jesus told His disciples this parable just after explaining to them the Parable of the Sower (Matthew Chapter 13, verses 1 to13). Both parables are directed at Christians.

In the Parable of the Sower, the LORD speaks about different kinds of persons who *heard* the word, but received it differently.

Each of the groups obviously professes love for the word, but the word profits their lives depending on the state of their hearts. Some people sit in the pews in

Churches all over the world every week, hearing the messages from God's ministers concerning their lives. However, not all of their hearts are fully yielded to the Holy Spirit.

Some are too set in their ways to allow the word of God penetrate their hearts, and treat the word of God as mere entertainment, they are wont to howl and shout as the Minister preaches the word, but as soon as they leave the church, they return to their own ways.

Some others are 'ghost' Christians, they hear the word, but they lack understanding of the word, and make no effort to ask further questions or study the word.

Some are too set in their ways to allow the word of God penetrate their hearts

"Therefore, they are ever learning,
and never come to the knowledge of the truth."
(2Timothy Chapter 3, verse 7).

Another group represents those churchgoers who are so entangled with the affairs of life, ambitious for money, wealth, fame, influence and worldly achievements, that they treat the word of God like a fairy tale.

They feel the need to show up and give the impression that they are Christians, but in their hearts, they think they know better: why rely on prayers when your connections can do it for you.

They KNOW that money answers all things! Therefore, for such people, the word of God may be music to the ears or warmth for the heart, but it is not sufficient for the 'real world.'

Unfortunately, they are the ones Pastors sing their praises because they are the big givers, the 'backbones' of the church! They are the ones Ministers try not to offend with their sermons. They are the main reason the church has become so lukewarm!

Thank God for the group that earnest thirst and hunger for the word of God that run with the earnestness of the Gospel!

They are the light and salt of the earth; they are the true church that Christ will come back to receive to Himself.

The Parable of the Wheat and Tares ties up the fate of everyone that proclaims to be a Christian. The LORD has

They feel the need to show up and give the impression that they are Christians, but in their hearts, they think they know better: why rely on prayers when your connections can do it for you.

allowed everyone to continue to coexist as 'Christians', ostensibly worshipping God together, 'in spirit and in truth'.

The presence of the tares in the body of Christ constitutes an on-going test that every true Christian must pass on the way to Heaven.

Tares have a way of looking more luxuriant than the wheat! Indeed, they might actually be mistaken for the real thing!

The wheat might even begin to envy the lifestyle of the tares, and to wonder why they seem to be the ones enjoying the 'blessings' of God! However, the Bible enjoins us:

Tares have a way of looking more luxuriant than the wheat! Indeed, they might actually be mistaken for the real thing!

"Do not love the world or the things in the world. If anyone loves the world, the love of the Father is not in him. For all that is in the world – the lust of the flesh, the lust of the eyes, and the pride of life - is not of the Father but is of the world. And the world is passing away, and the lust of it; but he who does the will of God abides forever" (1John Chapter 2, verse 15 to 17)

The time of the great harvest is at hand, when the tares will be separated from the wheat. The tares will be bound in bundles and burnt, while the wheat will be gathered into the LORD's barn.

11

හ FRUIT WORTHY OF REPENTANCE രു

PROVERBS CHAPTER 30, VERSES 11 TO 14

"Then he said to the multitudes that came out to be baptised by him, 'Brood of vipers! Who warned you to flee from the wrath to come? Therefore bear fruits worthy of repentance, and do not begin to say to yourselves, 'We have Abraham as our father.' For I say to you that God is able to raise up children to Abraham from these stones." (Luke Chapter 3, verse 7 to 8)

This was the stark warning of John the Baptist to the Jews who were trooping to be baptised by him in the River Jordan. This statement painted a graphic picture of the state of the nation whom God had chosen as His special people. They had become wayward, wild and worldly, by covering up with a veneer of being God's children by virtue of being descendants of Abraham.

This warning is also very apt for today's church. Many people masquerade as Christians but their lives depict neither the precepts nor the examples of Christ. The disciples of the LORD were first called 'Christians' or Little Christs, in Antioch because of their way of life.

The father of modern India, Mahatma Gandhi was famously quoted to have said to Dr. JH Holmes, Professor of Philosophy at Swarthmore College and a member of the Society of Friends, who had several opportunities to converse with Gandhi:

"I like your Christ; I do not like your Christians. Your Christians are so unlike your Christ."

Continuing in Gandhi's words, Dr. Holmes said, **"I believe in the teachings of Christ, but you on the other side of the world do not. I read the Bible faithfully and see little in Christendom that those who profess faith pretend to see."**

What damning verdict from someone whose total conversion to Christianity could have changed the history of the world! Is the situation different today? Would the verdict of disinterested observers be different concerning our general conduct as Christians today? This calls for sober reflection. I would recommend the prophecy of Joel to us today:

"Consecrate a fast, call a solemn assembly; gather the elders and all the inhabitants of the land into the house of the LORD your God, and cry out to the LORD. Now, therefore, says the LORD, 'Turn to Me with all your heart, with fasting, with weeping, and with mourning. So rend your heart, and not your garments; return to the LORD your God, for He is gracious and merciful, slow to anger, and of great kindness; and He relents from doing harm. Let the priests, who minister to the LORD, weep between the porch and the altar..." (Complete it please) Joel Chapter 1, verse 14, and Chapter 2, verses 12 to 13 and verse 17.

The subject of repentance covers virtually all pages of the Bible. God calls on His children to turn back from their evil ways and seek His face. He enjoins us to reject the customs and gods of this world and cling to Him, to trust Him and to walk according to His precepts and His commands.

The church today lives on the presumption that God's Grace is sufficient; therefore, we can continue to practice our 'faith' as we like.

Many people masquerade as Christians but their lives depict neither the precepts nor the examples of Christ.

The measuring rod is already stretched out; the LORD is measuring the depth of our faith and commitment to Him. He is coming for a Church whose garment is pure and white, without stain or wrinkle.

The Urgency of Now

The best day to have repented was yesterday; the best next day is today. Nobody knows when the trumpet will sound, when the children of God will be taken away. We must live our lives as if today is our last day on earth. Death is inevitable, and it can happen to anyone at any time. It is appointed to man once to die, and after that, judgment.

The church today lives on the presumption that God's Grace is sufficient

At the individual and corporate level, the Church - the body of called-out people needs to turn back to God as a matter of urgency. The night will soon come, when no man can work.

ෲ ABOUT THE AUTHOR ൪

Godwin Emeke Morka retired as Director, Research and Programme Development of the National Agency for the Prohibition of Trafficking in Persons (NAPTIP), Nigeria, in March 2021 after 17 years of meritorious public service. He is a Member of the Nigerian Institute of Computer Forensics and a Fellow of the African Institute of Strategic Managers.

He was called to the pastoral ministry in February 1995, and was ordained as a Pastor in Upper Room Baptist Church (URBC), Lagos on 30th October 1997. He served as Pastor at various parishes at various times between February 1995 and March 2006, and became the Rector of the Upper Room Bible College. He also served Church's Bible Study and Training Secretary.

On relocation to Abuja, he became a Member of First Baptist Church, Garki, Abuja, where he has served as Sunday School Teacher, Discipleship facilitator, and Director Christian Training Programme among other assignments.

Pastor Morka, an ardent student of the word of God and one who believes strongly in sound doctrine undergirded by faith holds an MBA and Post-graduate Diplomas in Theology from the Upper Room Bible College and the Nigerian Theological Seminary Ogbomosho, respectively.

He is married to Judith, and they are blessed with children and grandchildren.